T0066791

GROOMING
THE
INDIAN
MALE

Its all about meaningful companionship

GROOMING THE INDIAN MALE

SURABHI BANERJEE

PARTRIDGE

ISBN: Hardcover   978-1-4828-7482-2
               Softcover   978-1-4828-7481-5
               eBook   978-1-4828-7480-8

Print information available on the last page.

To order additional copies of this book, contact
Partridge India
000 800 10062 62
orders.india@partridgepublishing.com

www.partridgepublishing.com/india

This book is dedicated to my father, Mr Anil Chandra Maitra, who celebrated his 92nd birthday on the 11th Feb. 2016. He is a criminal lawyer by profession. He has been like a light house throughout my life. He has taught me to believe in my dreams & follow them with patience & perseverance.

A successful lawyer, great social worker & philanthropist, he has made it possible for our city to have the only auditorium, it has, which was badly needed.

He has donated his complete library of law books to the bar council of his city.

He has authored three books in our national language.

He has made us proud by winning many awards in many areas of his work.

I am extremely proud to be his daughter.

Contents

Chapter I

Dreams, Dreams & Dreams

Sumit, my Chartered Accountant son left for London today. He has gone to do his Masters in International Banking & Finance on full scholarship. We, as a family, are extremely proud of his achievements & I have been announcing this in a true Indian Mother fashion to anyone and everyone, who cares to listen.

After saying bye to him, amidst a barrage of instructions of dos & don'ts at the airport, we have just returned home. Now the reality has finally struck us, the complete family is feeling totally lost without him. He was the apple of my eye for the last 25 years.

My entire day's time table revolved around him. Now suddenly, this void.

I tried to draw solace from the fact that this is the story of each household today. What then is so different in my case. I tried to lighten my mood by thinking of good times, that we have had together for so many years. I told myself, "My son is a smart boy, who has gone to the city of his dreams, then what is my apprehension about?" A small voice asked me from within, "Have you really been able to equip him with the qualities that he would require to lead the life of a global citizen?" I did not get a convincing answer.

I have always observed that whenever I am confused, the wonderful, affectionate faces of my parents come in front of my eyes. Today, when I was feeling clueless, the same thing happened. Before I knew, I started seeing my own childhood in a flashback. These memories luckily brought a smile on my face. I saw myself as a naughty child, always busy playing some prank. The eldest of the three siblings, I was doted upon by both my mom & dad. Belonging to an affluent family & being the favourite grandchild, I never had to bother about doing any household chores. Education was given a lot of importance in my family. Ours was a family of lawyers & doctors, so I had the opportunity of doing my Masters in Science. Soon after this, my parents announced that my marriage has been fixed to a very handsome engineer, belonging to a very reputed family. So, at the age of 21, my life in my parents' place was over.

I entered a new era of my life & started learning to set up my own household. Within an year & a half, I was the proud mother of my son, Sumit – a wonderful, healthy, happy & naughty child. In this way, I stepped into the role of a mother.

Today, after 25 years, I was wondering what tra ining did I have, for playing the most vital role of my life. The role of a mother. What were my references? Whom was I trying to emulate, whenever I was instructing my child? I realised, unwittingly I was copying my grandma & my mother. They had done, what was best or rather, the social norms then. My question to myself was, is it applicable today, when I was bringing up my son? These thoughts started tormenting me. I wished I could turn the clock back, for the full 25 years. Once again, the voice asked from within, what different would you do? You would still have no clue, as to how to bring up a child. It is not about food, clothing & shelter, but so many other subtle things, which makes a real emotionally groomed personality. A really competent individual, who feels at ease & is confident, wherever he goes.

I thought, may be if I pen down my take on this, it could be a priceless gift to all the mothers to be, who aspire to groom the perfect Indian male with all the grace & charm, which will make him a wonderful companion to whoever meets him.

So, dear son, thanks a lot for training me through all my trials & tribulations, which I went through, while bringing you up & inspiring me to document my memoirs.

Chapter I

Dreams, Dreams & Dreams

Does this sound familiar?

Your take:

Chapter II

Electronic connections

E-mail has become our life line now. My day begins by checking my mail, hoping to see some thing from my son. Needless to say, it ends with an e-mail from me, instructing Sumit on various things. I am curious to know everything about his set-up there. I wouldn't mind getting a minute by minute update of his day. Well, he obliges by telling me about his flat mates. They are four of them sharing a flat. Luckily, they are all men. I had insisted, "Please do not share the flat with a girl" – I knew that was the norm there. Somehow the very thought made me paranoid.

Sumit keeps talking about his roommate, Rahul, who is a software engineer. He is always busy, working overtime in the office. He always seems to have some deadline or the other, which he needs to meet. His boss raises an eyebrow if he wishes to take a Saturday off.

Then he told me about Puneet, his second flatmate – a guy from Amravati, who is married, but is in no hurry to bring his wife here. He is also steeped in work in his office. He prefers to come home as late as possible. Sumit says, he takes pride in calling himself a workaholic and who has no other interest in life.

His third flatmate is Raj from Sangli. A Computer engineer, a topper in his college. He makes a lot of money. His only passion is face book. Loves to click selfies & post them on face book. The thing, which he likes to boast the most about is, the number of friends he has on face book. Yesterday, he announced the number to be 500. His aim is to make it to 1000 by the month end.

I was really impressed. I asked Sumit, then in that case, his friends might be visiting him every day. They must be having a great time on weekends, going out together, visiting new places etc. Sumit gave a big laugh, he explained, "Maa, these are face book friends, friend's friend & the huge chain. Raj doesn't like to meet people. He is an introvert, quite shy.& reticent. On the weekends, he loves to sleep for hours on end.

I did not know what to make of this generation. They were in one of the best cities of the world. They were earning good money & they were young. But none of them seemed to be really interested in living life. Their question was, what do I do with myself, if I come back early from office. Puneet says, "what exactly can I talk to my wife every day". All these reactions again made me wonder, what is the missing link? Why this apathy?

Once again I felt the boy is not to blame – what was his childhood like. What were the values, with which, they grew up?

Chapter II

Electronic Connections

What does this connection mean to you?

Chapter III

Food for Thought

These questions started flooding my mind, I wondered:

1. Whose territory is it?

2. Who should bell the cat??

3. Is there anything wrong the way they are?

4. What is it that is missing?

5. Are they to blame?

6. Is it really possible to bring a tangible change?

7. Will it hurt their ego, or they would love to learn?

8. What will be the biggest benefit if some change really takes place?

9. Who will enjoy the most?

10. Do Indian men really grow up to become extremely self centred?

11. Do they even realise the power of being emotionally well groomed?

12. What is it that, if they consciously make an effort to do, will make them really happy?

13. Do they have any expectation from their counterpart?

14. Do they even realise that life can be so much fun if they could share some time together, doing what interests them both?

15. What is it that is required to make an Indian couples life more interesting?

16. Have the Indian movies of the 60's-- 80's spoilt the Mind- set of the Indian Male, where they expect their Life partner just to serve them breakfast & pack lunch, give their handkerchief & wallet, & consider this ritual to be an epitome of romance?

Chapter III

Food for Thought

Is it really possible to bring tangible changes? How? :

Chapter IV

Unanswered questions.

All these thoughts kept playing on my mind & I started wishing someone had answered these questions of mine, long long back, when I was a mother to be. When my mind was at an impressionable stage, when I was so eager to learn & do things, that would help my child. Back then, all that I read was books on - how to handle an infant.

I spoke to Sumit about this, he thought over it, and said, in his mischievous way "give it a try - pen down your thoughts, who knows, some guys may turn out to be smarter than the rest, & become more adept at handling their life better."

My son as usual got me thinking.

I wondered - Well first things first.

Whose Territory is it?

Who really does have the power to start the moulding process?

This took me down the memory lane once again. I realised mind has its own way of handling tricky questions. I found myself transported back to a kitty party in Mrs. Verma's drawing room. We were 10 of us having tea together. I could actually recollect our conversation.

Now when I look back I realise, every age group has a common topic of discussion,

We were no different. Our favourite topic was our kids.

So, here's how it generally went -

Mrs. Verma - Oh! Did I tell you about my Rahul, he is such a darling, he just can't do anything without me. I have to be at his beck & call all the time.

Mrs. Sharma -- at least Rahul must be eating his food himself, my Varun - I tell you, he is in 4th standard now, but I have to run after him all over the house, just to feed him his lunch. She was looking at us expectantly, for our reaction.

All the other ladies joined in the laughter & commented; still you don't seem to lose any weight. Every time you look a bit healthier.

Mrs. Sharma - retorted tongue in cheek, « who cares? I am not one of those mothers, who would keep themselves busy in the Gym for physical fitness, at the cost of letting the child eat on his own."

Now when I think back, I realise, this is the vein in which all my peers spoke.

The answer to this kind of thought process is coming to me now.

I understand the underlying reason -

My take on it is as follows:

In the Indian society, which is a patriarchal society, the male child is considered the darling of the family.

So then, What are the perks that he enjoys?

1. Mother takes immense pride in pampering the child, by doing everything for him, and announcing proudly, in front of her friends- "Oh my Raaj, he can›t do a thing without my help. Ask him to take a glass of water for himself, he is sure to drop it & create a mess. I insist on giving him everything that he wants myself.

Why does she? Answer is very simple. -

Mothers self gratification.

2. I remember friends discussing over phone, how they remain busy every moment of the day - after Raaj finishes his school homework, with his mother's help, his mother takes immense pleasure in tidying up his table & putting back things in order.

Now I wonder, why does she do this?

According to me - it is the great Indian mothers' psychology, that of eternal sacrifice.

She loves to imagine herself as the martyr, who sacrifices her whole life attending to each & every whim of her son. In her own eyes, she rates herself as a good mother, only if she has been doing all this, at the cost of neglecting herself totally.

Now the question that came to my mind was, then, when does she get time to spend with her husband? Or have the need to enjoy, some personal moments with him?

For example plan something exciting, just for the two of them.

It dawned upon me, It is considered a taboo in her own mind, for the simple reason, the husband never expresses the need to have fun time with her. On the other hand the children are forever demanding, for more & more help in whatever they were doing

———•❧•———

Chapter IV

Unanswered questions

Anything wrong in being at the beck & call of your child?

Chapter V

Companionship! What for?

O ur kitty parties continue.

The topics have not changed much in principle, but yes there is a slight shift.

We all have reached our 30's. Our need for our husband's companionship has reduced a little more. He has grown in stature in his work life. He feels it is only justified, that he concentrates more on his work. After all for whom is he working so hard, is it not for his children?

Now the ladies talk more about college life for their children. They keep telling each other, how hard they are working for their son', to get into some dream institution, which will suit their own status. This then is the topic of discussion in the kitty parties.

Finally the son has entered his college life.

The mother's aspirations have soared once more. She wants to see him as her hero.

She imagines him doing everything, which she wishes her husband would have done, when they had just started their married life. This then Spurs her even further, to dedicate even more time, just to fulfil, all her son's many times unjust demands.

Son by this time, has become smart enough to understand, that the only hobby, which the mother has nurtured till now is, to be at the constant beck & call of her son. So he feels, if he stops ordering his mother around for everything that he needs, his mother would feel deprived of her proud privilege. This, he feels would make her feel really depressed & dejected.

So, by now he is convinced, it is not expected of him to tidy up his room or pick up his own soiled clothes, or put his shoes at the right place. He knows, either the servants, or mother or sister will do it. So why bother?

What does all this lead to? What then is the net result of this type of upbringing --

1. He is clueless, as to how, he is expected to manage his life, without his mother, as his personal manager.

2. The second scenario is, if he happens to be in a hostel, then his life centres around his studies, & fulfilling his own needs of having fun. This of- course goes without saying, using his father's bank balance. For, here earn while you learn, is not the norm in middle class families.

All the above factors then make me wonder, that with this kind of setting for the initial years of his life, where is the scope of honing his social skills?

Now the question is, what are "social skills".

Social Skills

What is it that comes to our mind, when we hear these two words? I kept thinking a lot, what it means to me. I realised that, I was thinking, "that I was thinking", but actually I caught myself "Day dreaming". I accepted in all humility that well! All that I craved to do these days, was keep on imagining different scenarios, or you could say I kept doing

Creative visualisation. So this is what I saw -

I was imagining a scene, where the man has developed interest in many things.

For example, from childhood he has been exposed to different forms of music. He has a habit of enjoying and appreciating music. He is able to explain to anyone, who feels interested to know, why this piece of music is beautiful.

The mother & son or the whole family enjoys sitting together, maybe twice a week or so, listening to different types of music - replaying certain parts, having a discussion & enjoying together. I asked myself, what will be the benefit?

A visual flashed in front of my eyes - I saw, all the family members were looking forward to this quality time, which they spend together. Each one wanted to finish off their individual work fast, so that they could sit together, smile together, relax together. For music has that supreme quality of giving peace, which is totally different, one can say un-adulterated. We in India call it "Nirmal Anand". It creates a sense of well being for people, who understand its power & beauty.

My mind fast forwarded itself to a scene quite a few years from now, a time when the children have left for higher education. They have gone abroad. They have gone far away from their doting parents. Suddenly the parents hear some particular piece of music playing on the Television. This brings back nostalgia of those beautiful moments-

Priceless moments which the family had spent together, when the children were home. These cherished memories brought back a broad smile on the parent's faces.

They were transported back in time. They felt an urge to call up their son & share the feeling. The son also responded so warmly & said, "Yes I remember, it used to be so wonderful, enjoying together." He went on to say, "I have downloaded many of those songs, some of our favourite music pieces & I hear them, whenever I feel homesick. It makes me feel better immediately."

I came out of my stupor & started wondering, what is it that needs to be done, to make this a reality? The answer that came was very simple.

Children need to be impressed upon, that it is also their duty to contribute towards making the atmosphere in the house beautiful. They need to take special efforts to liven up the atmosphere &. Not just use the house as a parking space. This is just one thing, what else can bring happiness? I wanted to ponder over this question.

Chapter V

Companionship! What for?

Does the companionship of your better half really matter?
Can Social skills be learnt?

Chapter VI

Different people, Different needs.

I decided to go for a long walk, on my own. I set out with different thoughts related to happiness, clamouring for attention. Suddenly I found my colony friend walking by my side. She is one person, who loves to talk. She asked me, so, what were you thinking about just now? You seemed to be lost in your thoughts. I gave a bland smile and said "nothing really" "why don't you tell me, what is going on in your life?, your life is always so interesting, I said".

Sarita was waiting to get this chance, she started of immediately. "you know how much energy I spend monitoring, my maid servant, when she is cleaning the kitchen. I hate to clean up any mess created on the kitchen platform. My son Aditya just does not respect this wish of mine. All that I want from him is, that he should tell me, if he wants a cup of tea or Maggie, tell me she said, how much time would I need to make it for him? But, no, he gets some wild ideas, that he would like to make MAGGIE on his own.

You can well imagine the result, How does he know how to go about it? A boy who has been brought up like a Prince since childhood, where I have catered to all his whims and fancies, being at his beck and call 24 / 7. Suddenly decides to act all self sufficient. Sure enough the whole kitchen was in a mess. He obviously cannot imagine cleaning up the working area, once he has finished using it.

So naturally there was a big row, in the house. He got upset, I became angry having to do the cleaning myself, as the maid would come only next morning. I have decided to report this to his father once he comes home from office. Aditaya should never try to work in the kitchen. After all he is a boy and he should behave like one.

I kept listening to all this with careful attention. I asked softly does your husband also create a mess, when he makes a cup of tea for himself? Sarita couldn't stop laughing at my question. She said "are you serious? Can you even imagine my husband working in the kitchen? He wouldn't even know where what is kept. No, No he loves to order me around the moment he is back. By this time we both had reached home. So we parted.

Once again the what if situation, cropped up in my mind. I thought, suppose the mother has an inherent need to enjoy her children's company on Sundays. She has to finish her cooking for the family anyway. So she gets her son interested in helping her in the kitchen, doing insignificant chores while the mother and son keep chatting, narrating funny anecdotes to each other. At the same time, child is observing his mother's style of cooking working in the kitchen, and he feels really fascinated with the whole process. The simple reason being, he loves his mother's cooking.

His mother tells him, she is feeling really tired, can he make a cup of cold coffee or lemonade for both of them. She teaches him how to make it by just giving him instructions and allowing him to do it. He has still not touched the gas burner, yet he has made something on his own. The satisfaction which the child feels is immense. His self worth goes up even further, when he hears his mother boasting about him to her friends on phone.

This trend continues, now Ajit is a teenager. He finds cooking some easy recipes very relaxing. Now a new interest has developed, off and on he looks up on U tube, cookery shows etc and tries out new but simple healthy recipes, which are not so time consuming. Sunday mornings have become very exciting, he takes his younger sibling into confidence and both are happily making a special menu for lunch. No more sitting in front of the T.V. for hours on end. Both the parents get sometime for a change to spend with each other. Sometimes the mother also joins in and helps in improvisation of the recipe. Father does not wish to be left out, He too offers to lay the table. The whole family is happily engrossed in preparing the Sunday lunch.

What is the net result?

Special bonding between the complete family. Happy memories left behind. The child has ended up learning basic culinary skills for the future. Th parents feel so satisfied and reassured that, their child will not be left at the mercy of burgers and outside food everyday no matter where life takes him in future.

Chapter VI

Different people, Different needs.

Developing culinary skills – how does it help?

Chapter VII
Times have changed

We constantly hear, times have changed. Nothing is, as it was before.

I was introspecting, what has actually changed, if we look at the family scenario.

At that very moment my phone rang. I picked it up. My close friend Vimla a home- maker like me was calling. We are great friends since so many years now. She said, "I have a suggestion to make & please don't oppose it"

This was her way of avoiding any kind of discussion, when she wished us to do something her way. I smiled & said, "Well! Since your mind is already made up-tell me what do I have to do". She felt relieved & said, "well! Now onwards, we are not going to have our kitty parties at home, we will select different Restaurants & have our parties there. This will then save us the botheration of bringing out our crockery, invite people home, cook & what not."

She was really thrilled, with her own idea. Prima facie, it made sense. Money was not an issue. We had our husband's earnings at our disposal. I agreed, said o.k. We met up for lunch the next day. 10 ladies together, can they just sit & eat quietly?

The manager had given us a nice corner, where we could make as much noise as we wished to. So like this our party started.

I took this opportunity to broach the subject, which was playing on my mind.

I asked them, as to what each one of them thought, about what has changed in our family system?

Rita said - we are free from the drudgery, which our mother's faced. We no longer stay in joint families. We can choose whether to cook or not. Order food from outside at will. We are not answerable to any elder member in the family. For me that's a great change she said.

Seema - we can go on watching T V serials, for hours on end. Make two minutes Maggie, for the child, when he comes home from school, if we wish to do so.

This is true emancipation she said. Answerable to no one.

Vimla joined in by saying, we are enjoying this freedom of having kitty parties in Restaurants, what more can we ask for in life?

The conversation continued in the similar vein.

One of our friends asked, but are we really happy? Do we miss anything?

Suddenly the light banter stopped. We all became a bit quite.

My friend Reema, who is a bit shy, said, "I feel we all miss companionship"

We all are very lonely. We have nuclear families. Most of us have either one child or at the most two. We don't like interference, so elders can't stay with us.

We chose not to pursue any career, since we thought motherhood meant catering to the whims & fancies of our child all the time we stopped thinking about ourselves as individuals. We were always fed the thought that, our happiness lies in the happiness of our family. She went on to say, there is nothing wrong with this statement, but we out of sheer laziness & cushioned life provided due to our husband's earnings, hid behind this concept. We did not strive to do anything, using our education & the time that we had at our disposal. So today nobody seems to have time for us. There is not much, that we do together as a family. She said "I wonder! Why my son Chetan should miss me, when he goes away.?"

Suddenly we all became very pensive. Anyway - we changed the topic as the waiter came with the bill & we had to pick up a slip & decide whose turn would be the next to throw a kitty party. What should be the venue?

After half an hour we started back for home. Once again while sitting in the car alone

My mind started conjuring up my favourite. "What if" situation.

It came to my mind, children these days are out of the house, during the college days. They keep roaming around with friends all the time.

What if, because of the simple reason, that the child has a special bond with his mother, he feels the urge to keep his eyes open, for all kinds of fun activities happening in the city.

He selects some musical programme, which may be has a free entry. A play which is being talked about a lot. A movie, whose rushes, his mom has been seeing on TV.

Maybe a new eating joint, which could be a novelty, yet suit the family budget.

He takes interest, plans an outing, taking his mother into confidence. It may happen, this being something new for the father, he shows some attitude & says, I don't feel upto it, you all go ahead.

The son &. Mother actually do that & have a great outing together. For quite a few days, after that, during dinner times they are narrating small anecdotes related to the outing & laughing.

The father soon realises, there is no fun in missing out on these outings. May be they could be really interesting. So next time he quietly agrees to join.

All of them are really excited- the tickets have been booked in advance & they had a great evening together. This brought a sense of fulfilment to the entire family.

What was the net result?

Emotional bonding between the family members became much stronger.

The child's net worth in the eyes of all the family members has gone up many times more.

He has become, "The Neighbour's Envy Parent's pride".

Chapter VII

Times have changed

Doing things together – any benefit?

Chapter VIII

One day outings

It has become a ritual. Every year once after every member has had a chance of arranging a kitty party, at the venue of her choice, we go for a one day picnic. By now we have exhausted our list of all the nearby places that we could visit & return back the same day. For all said & done, we are all good conscientious mothers, who think about nothing but our own family members all the time, so staying out one full day away from the family was indulgence enough...

This time we decided to visit Fort Jadhav Garh. We really loved the ambience, the food, the setting everything. But then we realised age was catching up on us. This being a fort we had to climb up & down all the time. All of us are complaining of knee problems, leg ache of various intensities. This movement part we were finding a bit too tedious. So we sat in the garden. Many of us were finding it difficult to sit down on the lawn. So we asked for chairs. All these things made us ponder over our situation.

Rita said, these outings are becoming a bit troublesome these days.

Seema joined in saying, my husband was complaining, "he said don't you all think spending so much for a one day outing is really a waste of lot of money.? She went on to say, and now after returning home in the evening, when I will complain of backache, I will really have a lot to answer.

Most of the ladies for once, were of the same opinion. They chirped in dialogues of similar nature, which they said they would have to hear at home, once they returned.

So finally we came to the conclusion- soon we would have to sit at home & think of entertaining ourselves indoors. These outings had lost their initial charm.

Once again ladies being ladies, started discussing what it is like when they are at home, on days when all family members are there. How boring it was. Husband was glued to the TV. watching News channels. Son was busy on his phone, locked up in his room. The door would open only when, some friend had fixed up some activity, outside the house. Then, within no time, he would get ready & rush off to meet his friends. So much for a weekend with family.

Then others commented, but then let us be honest, "what can they do with us anyway, just sitting at home? It becomes so boring."

One of them said on top of that my husband keeps complaining about how much money Sujeet is spending as pocket money. Does he even realise how hard I have to work to provide him that.

I was listening carefully and thinking, what each one is saying is so true. I asked myself was there no other solution? Did family time at home, really have to be like this. Each individual is an interesting person outside, with others. What happens when they are together as a family unit. Why is it so difficult to spend fun time amongst themselves as a family? My thoughts continued, soon it was time to return home.

We came back rejuvenated mentally but with a little bit of extra knee pain.

That night I observed my family members a bit more carefully. The whole night I kept tossing & turning, searching for answers to my own questions.

The question was, how to make life as a family more interesting, without going out all the time. I realised I had observed, the small children in our building sitting together in the play area of our building, playing interesting card games, sometimes board games.

Once again, I thought - what if, the child enjoys learning some interesting board games / card games & teaches them, with a lot of patience to his parents.

Then they look forward to spending lovely afternoons together, laughing, teasing cheating winning in these games together. The house seems to be filled with the sound of laughter & happiness. They do not even realise how the time flies when they are together.

They start looking forward to the next weekend. Each member tries to learn from their own peers.

They have a gala family time together. None of them seems to need their friends during these times.

Their friends feel quite curious, they ask, what is so interesting in your house, that you look forward to spending time at home. Small family trips of two to three days, have become so much more fun. They carry a bag full of games, wherever they go.

This helps them to enjoy the Resort even more. There is no time to get bored. They do not always need family friends to travel with them. They are so self sufficient, as a family now.

What is the outcome?

Parents feel, they are moving with the times. They have no time now, to go on unnecessarily sermonising their kids, for just about everything. Children develop a sense of well being & feel wanted in the true sense.

Chapter VIII
One day outings

How to make life more interesting as a family?

Chapter IX

Lap top my loyal friend

These days my friends & I have developed a new craze. We all wish to spend more & more time on the computer. Initially I used to sit & write mails. Now-a- days, that has reduced a lot. My son loves to read my mails, but prefers giving cryptic replies, such as 'oh,! Great mom, or very nice, or wow that must be fun. Or keep it up!

This is the general feedback I got from most of my friends, who wrote to their grownup sons. These were our friends from our community, but much elder to us in age.

I asked them, what do you do with your computer? Most of them said, "not much'

Just look up something on the net. But, anyway we are not so much interested in information of all kinds, so we play some games.

It struck me then, that. I had seen my son playing games on the computer as soon as he got some free time. Most of his games seemed senseless to me. They were about shooting down enemies etc. I told him one day we had a long weekend, coming up, can we plan a three day outing. He immediately answered (without even looking up, he was busy shooting some virtual enemy on the screen) go ahead, plan something & let me know. Please let it be some place interesting. His response once again transported me back on my 'Thinking. Track.'

I asked myself, why can't we as mothers get our teenage sons interested in selecting locations for these family trips? Anyway they are spending time on the computer.

What if, - He develops a hobby of looking up destinations worth visiting. He could have different folders, where he would have designed a complete package. Giving complete details, as to how many days would be required, the resorts where one could stay, the places worth visiting over there & and most importantly the amount of money that would be required to be spent.

I started day dreaming, I felt that a family which can inculcate, this kind of interest in the child, what could be the families gain?

According to me the Result would be, as follows-:

Many more meaningful outings, family vacations, depending upon the time available and finance availability, at that particular time.

I wondered how else would the child benefit?

This child's presence I felt would become indispensable, in the eyes of the family.

The child's awareness quotient would have gone up tremendously. For him ‹ ‹knowledge is Power ‹ would make more sense. Wherever he would go, amongst friends, relatives, elder generation, everyone would look upto him. He would be known as the 'Kaam ka Bandaa.' or you could say 'Most Wanted'

In the process he would get to see, so many beautiful places. His life would become an album of beautiful memories.

Chapter IX

Lap top my loyal friend

Your partner in excellence

Chapter X

Birthday, an important day of life

Today is 5th May. It is my friend Rita's birthday. We friends made it a point to wish her early in the morning. She thanked us but in a lack lustre manner. We were surprised. We finally rang up & asked her, what was the matter, why did she sound so low, was everything alright? She said, "Well, yes & no. Yes, because health wise we are all fine. But my husband is out of country and he is very poor in remembering dates. So, he forgot to call. My son had his college picnic, so he left in a hurry, early in the morning. So,

I am feeling quite low. My son forgot to wish me, he was in a hurry."

She tried to cover up by saying, "Of-course he did not do it purposely. He just forgot." I did not know what to say. I insisted she join me for lunch at my place. She agreed after a lot of reluctance. I started cooking for my friend, as my family had already left with their tiffin. My mind was, as usual engrossed – trying to find solutions. The questions that came in my mind were as follows:-

Q. 1) Would a wife forget her husband's birthday?

Pat came the answer, how could she? She would be planning since two days in advance, what all she would like to cook for him for that special day. She might like to visit a temple after he had left for office, where she would pray for his long & healthy life.

Q. 2) Can she forget her son's birthday?

No way. She would be planning a surprise party, gift & what not. After the child becomes a teenager, his birthday allowance demand would be increasing every year for his parties with his friends in McDonald or KFC etc. So obviously, the demand for money would have to go up. Anyway, forgetting his birthday was out of the question.

Then why could it be different when it was her birthday?

I realised that these sensibilities do not develop overnight.

Remembering important dates related to family members well in advance, making sure to buy meaningful cards, planning some small pleasant surprise for that day – all these things needed to become a family ritual. Something which the child needs to be taught from the time he was, may be, 6-7 years old. By the time he was 12 years old, this department should be made his responsibility. By now, the child would have started enjoying the process, as opposed to the mother's calling up close relatives on their birthdays and saying my husband & son both asked me to wish you on their behalf, since neither did they remember nor do they care.

Had the child been doing this, it could become the talking point for the family for the years to come.

A thought came to my mind, "What would this teach to the child?" He would be a little less self-centred. Get out of the world of I, me & myself, learn to take interest in livening up the life of his own family members. Net result – emotional happiness gained by the child would be priceless.

What more could be achieved through this, I kept asking. I felt may be the personal worries that the child (now a slightly grown up person) was facing, would fade away to a great extent, because many of them might have been baseless fears anyway. Mind when focussed on something else, gets refreshed and is automatically able to work better on the real issues at hand. It would be a complete win-win situation. I felt at peace within.

It gave me hope – such simple things when taught at the right time can make such a huge difference.

I fell asleep on this thought and the oppressive thought, which had started troubling me at the beginning of the day, by seeing my friend Rita's plight, gradually faded away.

Chapter X

Birthday, an important day of life

A day to be remembered by all near & dear ones

Chapter XI

Communication skills an enigma

As usual I went out for my morning walk today. A new advertisement board caught my attention. It said, "Teach your Child communication skills". I wondered, what exactly would they be teaching?

Teaching a language I can understand, but communication skills? I was intrigued. I immediately stored the phone number mentioned on the board and continued my walk.

I kept toying with the idea of calling up on this number and try to understand, what exactly the child would learn if they enrolled. I took an appointment and finally reached the institute.

A very pretty-looking receptionist welcomed me. I was asked to fill up a form giving all my personal details-like phone number, email id, whether I was employed, my husband's designation, his phone number, email-id etc.etc.

I was bewildered, I wanted to ask a few questions regarding the course which was advertised.

Anyway-finally I could request her to tell me what was meant by communication skills-that they wished to teach the student.

The receptionist looked quite bored then and just answered flippantly-,'Oh! They will stop making grammatical mistakes, maybe learn a few techniques for facing interviews. We will Video shoot while they are speaking and show them how ineffective they look while speaking! Maybe they will try to improve themselves..."

I was totally disillusioned. I came back feeling quite lost. I felt pity for the parents who would enrol their sons and daughters-hoping they will learn so many new things there. But feel totally dissatisfied once the course got over.

I wondered what was it that was bothering me. That night I got my answer while watching a Hindi serial on T.V.

A father in his 50's was complaining to his wife, I really don't know what goes on in our son Sanjay's mind. Whenever I ask him something, his answers are in mono-syllables. When he is on the phone, he can go on talking in hushed tones for hours on end.

I feel there is zero communication between us. The mother also joined in –My plight is not much different. He talks to me only when he needs to get his things done-like ironing his clothes, packing his lunch etc. He just sweet talks me into complying. The moment I wish to say something to him, he has a standard response -, "Just hold on-I am in a hurry, will talk later." That later never happens. Both of them looked quite dejected.

I started thinking, this cannot happen overnight. When did this emotional distance and communication gap start? What could have been done initially when the child was small, so that the scenario could have been different?

Once again my, what-if theory started in my mind. Would it be the same, if the mother herself had taken interest in reading Children's stories when he was small? Had taken interest in having a slot just before his bedtime (at the cost of sacrificing her TV serial time)for reading out a good short story-with some simple but profound moral?

Explaining the story and asking his interpretation regarding what he feels could be the moral. Both mother and son would laugh over it and have a consensus regarding the moral. Gradually as he would grow up, he would pick up books of his choice. Reading exciting, thought provoking good books would have become a need by then. He still would be sharing the companionship with his mother, but there would be a role reversal. He would be reading more contemporary books & explaining in a nutshell, what the book is all about, during may be, dinner time – the family time together. He would be motivating his mother to read some of these books. He would be presenting the 'must read' books to his parents. May be, would take it one step further – get the CD of the movie made on it. The whole family could be enjoying watching the movie together at home, using the 'surround sound' system, which the father might have gifted to the family for the same purpose.

What would be the outcome? A gratifying experience for the whole family. Animated discussions on the movie, each one's take on it etc. Expression power and communication skill would have developed naturally. He would have n number of things to discuss & talk about with his parents. He would never feel tongue-tied in front of anyone – any gathering. The family would feel so secure, since they would be aware of each other's thought process, so well. So many suicides could be averted, due to sharing.

I asked myself, would the parents still have to enrol their children to learn basic communication skills?

Chapter XI

Communication skills an enigma

When does the Emotional distance & Communication gap start?

Chapter XII

Gym – a social norm

The latest fad which we friends have developed now a days, is the fascination for joining a gym. Today, going to a gym has more or less become a status symbol. I decided to visit a gym, which is considered a 'state of the art' gym, very close to our house.

I went around 5 O'clock in the evening to just see once & get the feel of the place. I was waiting at the reception. I saw a lady with her teenage son. They seemed to be very angry at each other. Somehow I got chatting with the lady. She started complaining bitterly. Her grievance was that she was ready to pay the heavy fees for the gym for her son and he was just not interested in exercising. I asked her son why was he reluctant to join? He gave a very straightforward answer, "It is boring to go on doing sets of exercises repeatedly, every evening, there is no fun in being closeted in a closed area with blasts of AC, doing something so routine." I realised he had a point. I wondered what could be the alternative. The mother was right that exercise was important, but the son was right in his place too. I felt why do parents have to make everything their child does, a talking point for their drawing room. Why can't a child be observed in his childhood, as to what type of sports interests him, in what he seems to be good and then motivate him to learn the sport properly, through proper training. This would make the child look forward to his evenings. It would motivate him to finish his home work quickly and rush to the play ground. Playing in the fresh air would make him healthy & happy. Exercise would be taken care of naturally. Parents would not need to pay high amounts for gym membership.

I remember my childhood, when our neighbour Mr Sharma, a businessman would take his son, an 11 year old boy, to the ground to play football. On weekends, father & son would go for Table Tennis practice. The child would return home radiant with happiness. He would boast in front of us how many goals he had scored that day. How many games he won in TT against his father. Now after 15 years when the boy has become a grown up man & now works in London, came home to India last month. We were very fond of him. He came to meet us. We were talking about his childhood. He told us very enthusiastically that he still plays football for his Bank. He is the Captain of his team. He gets to visit different countries of Europe, when he represents his Bank for friendly matches with other branches. He said, we need to run a lot on the football ground, so I enrolled for London Marathon. This motivated me to practice running every day after office hours. He said this has helped me in making so many new friends of different backgrounds but similar interests.

He went on to say, thanks to Dad's enthusiasm in my childhood, I am able to maintain my physical fitness, while enjoying the sports that I love so much.

I realised this small effort taken by parents in the early years of the child's life can set the need for physical fitness for life. It becomes a basic requirement. The child develops a sense of sporstman spirit & learns the importance of being a team player. Learns the importance of making friends. This definitely makes him a very social person.

What if:

Parents learn to let go, they stop sermonising their children for everything. At least the physical fitness part is handled, with the sense of sportsman spirit, amongst the family members. This may be then, could become one point where it was not required to prove a point by anyone. It was done for the pleasure of seeing the happiness in the concerned persons eyes.

Chapter XII

Gym – a social norm

Physical fitness – something to look forward to

Chapter XIII

Conversations

Going to the Gym, somehow did not suit me, but exercising was a must. So I found my option of going for Yoga, early in the morning in a nearby garden. I really started enjoying the experience. There were many ladies of my age group. I got a chance to make many interesting friends. Over there I made a friend who works as a marriage Counsellor in the Family Court. She started narrating some of her experiences. The latest one she said was-a couple married just 6 months back had filed for divorce.

This lady told us the major grievance which this girl had. It was she said that -the man had nothing to say or share whenever they were having meals together or went to some garden or anywhere. Whenever she would say, why don't you talk something, he had a standard answer, I have nothing interesting to talk about. I do not have this habit from my childhood. You talk and I will listen.

Initially the girl ignored this and kept on chatting. Soon, she said, she started dreading his company. She said he loves to watch the news and the Stock market. Beyond that he likes nothing. Goes to office, comes back, eats... and that's it.

The man said, I really don't understand what exactly does she want me to talk about. I can talk to my friends and colleagues because we all enjoy talking about the Share market.

With her, she has no patience beyond a point!

I wondered why do some people become like this, when they are grown-ups? What went wrong in the initial years?

I started thinking, what kind of family could be labelled as a happy family?

The picture that flashed in my mind was so simple. A family of 4 --parents and 2 kids sitting for a meal together. The father starts narrating small funny incidents of his childhood. The mother joins in narrating her memories of pranks played by her in her childhood.

The whole family is in splits. The children being so innocent have no inhibitions, they too want to tell what happened in their school or playground. The parents were automatically encouraging the children to tell them in full details and were laughing and enjoying what the kids were saying.

These sessions in the family become extremely contagious. One incident narrated, reminds the other person something in the similar vein and before one knows the whole family has a gala time together. I wondered what would be the outcome of all this.

The answer came loud and clear. A lot can be learnt from each other's experience.

The learning that happens is of a very permanent nature. Its an age old proven fact that anything learnt through a story remains in one's mind for a much longer time. It is a long lasting impression.

For I realised, Good values are nothing, but impressions implanted in our minds during our Growing up period.

Is this all? Or there is something more that happens-Well!

1. The person becomes a much better conversationalist.

2. He always has N-number of stories to narrate, whenever he is among friends or colleagues.

3. He is an asset for any group. His wife actually looks forward to spending time with him.

4. He finds himself wanted & invited everywhere.

5. People find him to be very charming – and charming people are considered handsome.

For after all, "Beauty lies in the eyes of the beholder".

Chapter XIII

Conversations

Interesting narrations?

Chapter XIV

Children's summer holidays, Parent's nightmare

School holidays have started. The mothers are complaining, it is the nightmare period of the year. How to keep the child occupied, the whole day. Early morning swimming. But this gets over by 8 AM. Letting the children out in hot sun makes them fall ill. Evenings are booked at the Basketball club. Even after all this – the child seems to be restless all the time. He just can't sit at a place for even a few minutes. There is a lot of shouting & admonishing going on in the house. The child feels his mother is too much. She is always scolding him, don't do this don't do that. The mother, on the other hand feels my son is getting on my nerves all the time.

My friend Rohini, mother of two sons, who seemed to be at her wit's end all the time, seemed quite relaxed when I met her this time. I felt curious and asked her, "How did this change happen?" She answered with a broad smile, "Oh! I used to observe my sons, Tushar & Gaurav, they both seemed to enjoy the musical pieces, the background music of any song, more than the song itself. Many a time, they would be replicating the same music through their voice." She said, "I asked them, Would you all like to learn how to play this kind of music." They answered enthusiastically, "Oh yes, we would love to learn to play the keyboard(synthesizer). In that we have the option of playing all kinds of instruments." The whole family got excited. I located an established music class in a nearby area. We went there together. I had never seen my sons' eyes shine like this before. So many keyboards were arranged there. Children of different sizes were learning. There was an air of happiness in the air. I enrolled both my sons there. Now for 2 hours in the morning, they are happily occupied in learning music. After returning home, they love to practice on their personal keyboards.

They get appreciated in the class, the next day, and that means a lot to them.

Rohini said with awe in her voice, "They are literally transformed! They are much more well behaved, more polite & calm. It is a pleasure to have them around."

REALISATION

Listening to Rohini, I realised what she was saying was so true. Nothing can be more soothing than a child playing an instrument at home in his leisure time. It has the immense power to draw the family together and create a sense of bliss for these particular moments for the whole family. After all, what is the most cherished desire of every family? Is not a real family bonding, a great need?

We can say, it is like an Insurance Policy, which will help in holding the family together. It will enable them to enjoy wonderful musical evenings together.

Chapter XIV

Children's summer holidays, Parent's nightmare

Talents need to be discovered

Chapter XV
Gratitude, Oh! My God

I was feeling bored, sitting alone & watching TV. I called up my neighbour staying in the adjacent building. She was equally bored, sitting alone. She insisted I join her for a cup of tea. I agreed & went over. We are good friends, we really enjoy each other's company a lot. So we had a nice time sipping tea & watching our favourite serial together. After an hour or so, her son returned from school. He was tired, after a long day at school. He just threw his school bag down & after changing his clothes, wanted to rush off to the play ground. My friend Lalita asked her, "how was school?"

He made a long face and said "Oh! Today we had that most boring period."

I asked, which one? he answered, aunty it was Moral science. Every week we have to sit & listen to all kinds of senseless things, such as "be grateful to your parents, for all they do for you etc etc". Tell me aunty, he said, how artificial it would be, if we start feeling gratitude towards our parents, for whatever they are doing for us.

It is their duty anyway, so big deal. Saying this he rushed out to meet his friends.

Lalita & I kept looking at each other, wondering how to react. She said, with a deep sigh, I really don't know how to handle this. My son Rohan, really never acknowledges, what we do for him, he just takes everything for granted. Always points out how much more his friends get from their parents. He is always comparing with friends who are richer than us. He is never happy or satisfied with what we have provided for him. I could see sadness in her eyes.

It was getting dark outside, so I decided to leave. I reached home, but my friends sad eyes kept flashing in my mind. I wondered where had we gone wrong?

as parents, in inculcating such an important value in our children. I came home lost in my own thoughts. I saw a what's app message on my phone. My son had written "Rushing off to a thanks giving dinner, at my office colleagues place." this colleague was a British person, who had attended a Diwali get together at my son's place & wanted to include him for some, traditional celebration in his own house. This he explained to my son was actually meant to be attended by family members only. So getting included was a privilege.

This word thanksgiving, stuck to my mind. I started thinking is it not important to have some kind of a ritual, during some of our celebrations, where the children get to see how the elders in the family, acknowledge the other members of the family for whatever they have done for them.

I realised Birthday parties are the first important memories of every child. Since, he is the centre of attraction on that day. That is supposed to be his day. He expects gifts from everyone. These days even the maid servants, talk about celebrating their children's Birthday, by cutting the cake. We all seem to have picked up this ritual from the western countries.

Children from middle class families talk about return gifts, which they need to buy for their friends. This again is a source of competition, for the parents. They keep on planning as to, how they can give something more costly, than what their neighbours son gave. The whole conversation revolves around this for days on end, before the birthday.

I wonder, what if, we could encourage the child to sit with his family, on his birthday in the morning, for may be just half an hour & express himself. As to why he liked each & every gift that he got from his parents & grand parents that day. What it meant to him. A genuine heartfelt thank you, was said by the child. This would then become his habbit. When he would grow up, and start realising how much it takes to be able to provide, everything for the family members. He would develop a sense of gratitude from within. He would never find it in him, to compare his parents efforts, with the richer families.

This kind of despair which is seen in the eyes of parents, saying "we are never good enough, no matter how hard we try" would never happen. The whole point is, Yes! We are responsible for the situation, we are in now, because we did not have the foresight to teach them the importance of Gratitude.

It is rightly said, being a parent is no child's play.

Chapter XV

Gratitude, Oh! My God

Parents – Do they really need to be acknowledged

Chapter XVI

It's my life

Today in our book reading club - we decided to talk about self help books. One of the ladies made an introductory remark. These are books, which talk about success stories & help people to become more successful.

Due to this remark, we generally got into a discussion, as to what was the definition of success, for each one of us. We realised in a nutshell, it all boiled down to financial success. Who makes how much money, and what all luxury items, they can afford.

They all asked me what was my definition of success?

Frankly speaking, I had not given it a serious thought before. I used to feel every member in the family is an individual. Each individual's success story would be his personal success, based on his dreams, & ambitions. Today when all my friends were looking at me, waiting for my answer, I was surprised at the way my mind started working, & at what came out when I spoke.

Well! This is the thought that surfaced.

First of all, I felt that these lines "it's my life" does it really mean anything? Can anybody grow up from an infant to a grown up person, without the selfless support of his parents. For years on end. The parents put the needs of their children way above their own needs, to help the child make his dream come true. This could be, at whatever stage he might be, at that time. So suddenly how can it become "it's my life"

So I felt success also can be termed as a family success. I realised it was so important to keep a log of yearly achievements of the family. If at the beginning of the year, each member makes a wish list, noting down what all he wishes to do in that year. They all sit down & share with each other. They put down some, under family wish. For example - visiting some place, another country or renovating some parts of the house. Going for some famous Music festival together. It could be anything depending upon what the family likes. Then on the birthday of each family member, sitting down & taking stock, ticking off what all has been completed. Reframing what all, needs to be still attended to. At the end of the year basking, in the glory of the success, of all that, the family could complete together. This can be such a fulfilling experience. The whole family would feel so happy & truly successful. When years would have passed by, this ledger would be a priceless, Collection of memories & achievements. Each member would feel proud of his share in that.

Can there be a bigger form of success, for any family?

I was surprised to see that, there was pin drop silence in the room. All my friends were listening with rapt attention. I had got carried away by my own emotions.

We all wished, we had started something like this long back, when children were really small. Then

Sarika my friend, youngest of all, asked but, how would this really help?

I said, it's my belief, it would make the child develop a sense of humility & good cheer. He would understand the value of belonging to a good family. He would realise his family time was priceless. No matter how busy he became, he would always crave for this Union & make time for being with family.

All the above discussions pointed to one common factor, that the better part of a couples life is over in bringing up children.

What does all this culminate into?

Chapter XVI

It's my life

Humility & Good cheer – How does it help?

Chapter XVII

Foreign lands

Time to fly. 21 years have passed, we as friends of our kitty party & mothers of our children, (that was our real identity these day's. So & so's mother) now find that our topics of discussion are totally different.

Today we were discussing how time has flown. Finally the children have grown up.

The world has started beckoning them. We as parents also have a common talking point. Each one of us is informing, where our son is going for higher studies - USA, Australia, Canada, U k.

All parents have become extremely busy, mortgaging their properties, in order to make it possible for their son to leave, in search of greener pastures.

Tearful goodbyes are being said. Internet is becoming the lifeline. Now when we friends meet, we keep telling each other, how we maintain our schedules to be able to keep ourselves free, to attend our son's call. We have become well informed mothers, we know which country is ahead or behind by so many hours of India.

Initially the calls would be there everyday. Soon the children are settling down in their new surroundings, new routine, new friends & new found freedom. Now the calls are weekly once. We friends tell each other, this makes more sense, for there is nothing to talk about everyday.

In this manner some months, then years have passed. Now the story line in the drawing rooms have changed for us, as parents back home. Each one of us is narrating proudly, which all countries our children are visiting. Which all sports our children are used to now. Some talk of Ski - trips, others about mountain biking, some about running the full Marathon.

Faces of all the parents, are shining in borrowed glory.

Why this Glow?

This thought came to my mind when, I sat for my meditation early in the morning at 5A.M. When all was quite around. The answer was simple, it reflected that as parents, we have been successful in bringing up our children, to match up with the changing times.

They are successful out there, making the parents feel successful here.

Chapter XVII

Foreign lands

In search of Greener Pastures

Chapter XVIII

Learning from Peer groups

Today, after a long time, all of us decided to meet up for lunch. It was no one's birthday, neither was it a kitty party. We felt we have come a long way in life. We decided we would have a common agenda for this get-together. We considered ourselves to be really matured ladies, who understood a lot about life. The topic decided was – "Benefits of grooming the Indian male child"

We had a great time together. All the ladies had thought a lot, debated on the topic at home and come really prepared. We wished we had done something meaningful like this, when we were younger. Maybe we could have learnt so much through each others' view point & experiences. Anyway, better late than never.

So, this is the gist of what came out of our 4 hours of discussion. The consensus was:

As we are living in an era of equality, at least among the educated class, the expectations from the girl child are much more, right from her childhood. In every family, there is either one child or two children, at the most. Equal importance is given to both the siblings, regarding their education as well as general grooming. She is brought up as a complete independent individual. She can take care of all her financial as well as emotional needs. She is taught, not to be dependent in any which way on anyone.

So, the million dollar question was, what is the final outcome of this training?

The result is as follows:

We all agreed unanimously that –

1. A wonderful lady is created, who is adept at multi-tasking in the real sense. She has a huge sense of self-worth.

2. She finds it below her dignity to depend on any man to pay her bills.

3. She is capable of managing her office, as well as home front, in a very balanced manner.

4. She knows how to play the role of a beautiful host, when she has guests over at her place.

5. She takes pride in dressing up well & looks properly groomed & poised all the time.

6. She is aware, she has an important image to maintain.

This is today's woman – no more the "bichaari abla naari of yester years"

Chapter XVIII

Learning from Peer groups

An era of Equality

Chapter XIX

The other side of the coin

This, then led our discussion to the other side of the coin – "The version of today's Man". It somehow came to our mind that – The Man may still have remained the same. He may still be emulating his father, using his picture stored away in his subconscious mind as his role model. We asked ourselves, "Is there anything wrong in that?" Well! Not really.

We do need to respect our parents – that's what we are taught from our early childhood. We realised it was only natural for the son to emulate his father. The reason being – unknowingly, he would be inheriting genetically, many of his father's qualities. So anyway, by default, he would be behaving like his father in many areas of life.

Now the bone of contention was that –

The only thing we are all forced to remember, time & again is that "Change is the only constant factor in life". So what was right and considered great, yesterday, may not be appreciated in the same light today.

We all decided to analyse this statement categorically.

Q. What was the role of an Indian male till the previous generation.

1. He was the breadwinner. It meant that he was solely responsible for taking care of the complete financial security of the family. This included his parents and pitching in, as & when required, for his brothers & sisters as well.
   He had to play the role of a 'Noble-Man' provider for one & all.

2. Financial burden started increasing. It became more difficult to keep up with the rising rate

of inflation. In order to help the financial kitty of the family, the lady of the house took it upon herself to start working outside & start earning. She took up a job. Now she had to make sure, she was not neglecting any of her household chores. Not only that, she had to be eternally grateful to her husband for allowing her to take up the job.

3. Family members had a very different picture in their mind regarding a quintessential daughter-in-law. So many times they made it more difficult for this working lady. They kept on expecting and making demands on her precious time for doing mundane things, which anyway, they should have been managing on their own.

4. What would be the scene at the work front? Over here, her male colleagues would try to prove that she was more pre-occupied with her family problems, hence she should not be given promotion, because she would not be able to handle the added pressure. This meant that she had to be twice as good as many of her male counterparts in the office as well.

5. Everywhere the man had a right to give a condescending look to women and have a smug expression – "Let me see, how long she can manage and last under this kind of pressure".

6. What would be the scenario at home on weekends – i.e. Sunday or some holiday? Obviously the man would like to rest for a longer period in the morning. After waking up, expect his hot cup of tea to be ready & served. But then, not only that, being a holiday, should the wife not cook some extra delicacies? Mother-in-law would definitely expect a little bit more time & pampering from the daughter-in-law since she was available today. Everyone seems to be justified in their place.

7. Evening time – on a holiday, we were in a pensive mood. We were thinking what would be the thought process of a typical Indian male, would this thought even strike him that maybe, the wife needs a change. She would feel great if he would take some initiative and suggest some interesting outing, or express that he would like to take her out exclusively

for a nice dinner to a place of her choice or to a fancy place, which he has heard about. Will he ever dream of suggesting that she dress up really nicely. That he would like to spend the evening with her, eat good food & mainly talk about interesting things and not just about day to day mundane things? We all realised expecting this type of behaviour would be so much out of character or out of place, considering our Indian male psyche. He has never seen anything like this done by his own parents. His childhood memories are priceless – they are imprinted in his mind. Whenever he goes down the memory lane, he can actually see his mother going on cooking endlessly on all holidays, festivals and other occasions, see the satisfied look on his father's face, obliging her by enjoying the delicious food and may be, saying once in a while in public that nobody cooks a particular dish, the way his wife does. What was the impact of this? Mother would feel all the more enthusiastic about cooking some more.

The question that arises is what is wrong in all this? – Nothing – that is, if we could remain frozen in time.

But practically speaking, fortunately or unfortunately that is never possible for we all have to accept that – change, change & change is the only truth in life. We are all witness to the Darwin's theory, "Survival of the fittest".

Today, the era in which we are living – the society is witnessing so many divorce cases, living-in relationships are becoming the order of the day. We, as a society, need to ask, "Are these healthy signs?"

We, as Indians claim very proudly – strong family system, based on the successful institution of marriage is the backbone of the society. If that is so, can we take a lack lustre approach towards it and allow it to become hollow and as a result, collapse. You will all agree that will be a calamity. Nothing is lost even now. It is never too late, as we say in Hindi, "Jab jaago tab hi savera".

This is the wake-up call for all mothers, who wish to see their next generation to be truly happy!

Chapter XIX

The other side of the coin

The Noble man

Chapter XX

Life is beautiful

Life was beautiful

Life is beautiful

Life will always be beautiful. Tall claim, is it?

In my 60 years of life, I have realised one thing, time & again. Every problem has a solution. The only reason why we can't see beauty in our day to day situations, is because, we all have set ideas about how a particular thing should happen. The moment something goes out of line, our irritation starts. Then no matter what, we keep on complaining, but why did it not happen the way, I wanted.

Dear Readers! Won't you all agree, the Universe is under no obligation to follow our instruction manual all the time. It has it's own ways of meting out what it feels, is right in a given situation. Does it mean we remain helpless victims all the time? No – not at all – we are the biggest creation of the nature, we have been blessed by a priceless thing called MIND – we are our own masters, who can use our mind to take decisions, the way we want.

This reminded me of a small incident of my childhood – where I realised that, that really, smiling is a habit, which we consciously need to develop. I was in the 5th grade of my school. I used to always take pride in scoring full marks in English dictation test. This particular day, when the teacher was announcing the marks – she announced my marks as 98/100. My best friend who was always first in all kinds of sports events, had scored 5/100.

She burst into tears on getting her test paper. She kept on wailing—she would not be allowed to go for basketball practice for a month now, till she improved in her spellings. We could all understand, as basketball was her passion.

Then she looked at me and was surprised that even I was crying. She asked me, really touched, "You are crying for me, how sweet you are". I answered scornfully, why should I do that? She asked me in wonder, "Then why are you crying?" I said, "Just imagine, I lost 2 marks. Isn't that awful? Next moment she couldn't stop laughing. She said, "How vain can you be? Don't you like to smile & be happy when you have done so well? Do you really need to focus on the 2 marks that you lost?"

Somehow her simple logic hit me hard. I wiped my tears & really saw the beauty of the thing. I had unknowingly learnt a lesson for life!

It is really up to us to decide what we wish to look at, the dirt around us or at the twinkling stars in the sky.

Chapter XX
Life is beautiful

Beauty lies in the eyes of the beholder

Chapter XXI

It is never too late

Well, you have already read the simple tips, the small changes, the awareness that can help us, if we choose to implement them, step by step to create a lovely & satisfying life.

That would be possible only with the help of our efficient, capable, hard working, large hearted and full of life – sons & daughters. Our dear ones, of whom, we are really proud to be MOTHERS.

Chapter XXI

It is never too late

Can some change be initiated?

Anecdotes

Some real life anecdotes which make us sit back and think. We wonder, would they have still behaved in the same manner, if they had undergone the training mentioned in this book?

This is a real incident of a close friend Mr & Mrs Verma, they got married in the year 1979, on 6th April, obviously an arranged marriage. Marriage took place in M.P.

Mrs. Verma came with a lot of romantic expectations to Pune, with her husband. He was working in Pune. She kept on waiting with bated breath that soon he would suggest something about their honeymoon. Two months passed and no sign of any such suggestion. Finally she took courage and suggested that they go out somewhere for honeymoon. The husband agreed to take her on the following Saturday. The whole week passed with a perpetual smile on the wife's face. Finally, Saturday arrived. She had already packed her bag, complete with her husband's things for the weekend. Excited about the ensuing surprise which her husband had promised to give her.

Saturday evening, the husband finally called the rickshaw - both started, the lady with a beating heart, husband with a smug smile. He took her to Jungli Maharaj Temple on the Jungli Maharaj Road. Took out a bottle of honey, gave it to her & said, let's watch the moon together. He then enquired, "So, how did you like the honeymoon?" He had enjoyed his own prank to the hilt. The wife just kept staring at him. She returned home quietly, with tears in her eyes.

So -- that's a honeymoon.

Next 5 to 6 years passed in bringing up their only son. Then the husband suggested graciously - "Why don't you study Law?" She enrolled -- next year 4 years passed in studying & juggling household chores. No time for any light banter or emotional moments. The wife, by now had got seasoned to look out for her own entertainment with her other lady friends.

After 25 years, she felt why not go for a movie with the husband. This was, maybe the first time she put her foot down about an outing and took him for a very interesting movie, booked tickets in advance. Popcorn was purchased- both entered the hall. The movie started, popcorn got over- after an hour or so, the husband needed to go out- so he went. No sign of his return – the whole time the wife kept turning her head, looking out for her husband's return. The girls sitting next to her saw her discomfort and asked if they could help. She did not want to ruin their movie - though her's was definitely ruined - the movie was not making any sense anymore. Last 15 minutes were remaining - he suddenly came & joined her. Full of concern, she enquired, "Are you ok? Are you feeling ill or something?" Same smug smile & flippant reply, "No no, I just thought I'll explore the complete Multiplex building & see how it is made." Once again she was left speechless.

So much for companionship, "Till death do us apart."

Any suggestions? How should a lady react to these situations?

Does it remind you of any similar situations?

So this was Mr & Mrs Verma!

This is the story of Mr & Mrs Bose, married now for 20 years.

One day they were both standing on the footpath of the crowded Main Street of Pune. Suddenly there was a slight let up in the traffic, the husband decided to cross the road. He immediately grabbed his wife's hand & started literally dragging her quickly in order to cross the road, while in the process, he was thinking, "I wish my wife's hands were a bit more soft, they are so rough. I am sure other ladies must be having softer hands" (as told to us later).

After crossing the road, he turned sideways to scold her for walking so slowly. He was horrified to see - he had forcefully caught hold of the hand of a Muslim lady in a Burqa & dragged her. His wife at the same time, was standing on the other side of the road, trying to pacify the angry Muslim man (whose wife had been taken to the other side of the road) that it was a harmless mistake on the part of her husband.

What do you say to this?

Suppose in the early years of their married life, they had spent a few romantic moments, just sitting together in front of the TV, watching some programme of common interest, holding hands & sharing the warmth & each other's companionship. Do you think this would have still happened?

Just the feel of the hand would have prompted him to turn & see that this was not his wife, for his wife definitely has lovely soft hands, which, any man would love to hold.

Does this kind of romance really require so much effort?

I think it's a need, a senstivity -- it's either there or not there.

This is an interesting story of Mr & Mrs Joshi, married for 20 years. Mr Joshi took a lot of pride in bragging in front of his friends that his wife cooked non-vegetarian dishes really well. One day, he met his friends (who lived in the same building)in the parking lot of his building. Somehow it so happened that they decided to have a pool dinner. Only stags. He promptly announced he would make his wife cook chicken Biryani for all ten of them. His wife was a working lady, working from 10 – 7 pm in a Bank. This party day happened to be a Friday – a working day for her.

A day before, that is on the Thursday, the husband announced in a matter of fact manner that he had promised his friends that he would be bringing the chicken Biryani for the stag's dinner on Friday. The wife graciously answered, "Please go ahead order the Biryani wherever you wish". Home cooked Biryani was the attraction. The husband became all huffy & puffy – a serious fight followed. The wife made it very clear. She had an important meeting in the Bank, for which she needed to leave early & return late from office. Hence it would not be possible for her to make it. A cold war between the two ensued immediately from that moment, lasting nearly a month. The following morning, the wife was busy locking the main door before leaving for her office in a hurry. One of their neighbours, Mr Shinde walked upto her and expressed his condolence, saying he was extremely sorry to hear that her uncle had suddenly passed away. So, obviously, out of respect for her, the party had been cancelled. She was at her wit's end, wondering which uncle had passed away. She acted all sad & lost and left for office, wondering what all this was about.

Later in the evening, when she confronted her husband, he answered angrily, "what other option did I have?"

So dear Readers – so much for communication skills, or the basic need for understanding each other and communicating well!

What do these small silly things in life teach us? Don't they force us to sit back and think, what will be the impact on the children, who are growing up in this scenario in their family? They may laugh at it. Feel, may be, these are non-issues. But these are the small insignificant things, which shapes up the personality of the next generation.

They become really confused. They certainly do not like what they see.

They try to emulate what they see their western counterparts doing. After a point of time they find it does not go totally with their upbringing or what they believe in. This again creates a mess in their minds.

Hence to help our sons & daughters to be more grounded and confident about their social skills, it is so required to analyse the complete picture.

Start from the beginning – i.e. when the male child is born.

The biggest need of all members in the family is the need of companionship. This one thing can-not be got overnight. This bond requires a lot of nurturing and sensitivity of all concerned.

Anecdotes

Your own anecdotes, which make you laugh

About the Author

Mrs. SURABHI BANERJEE

Mrs Surabhi Banerjee is a mother of two very accomplished children – son, an Investment Banker in London, daughter, a practicing Architect in India. Husband, a Mechanical Engineer, is the backbone of her life. He has truly proved that behind every successful lady, is a man, who has a magnanimous heart. He is a person, who has always motivated her to dream, follow her dream & convert her dream into a reality. In the 38 years of their married life, everything that she has achieved, its only because of his support & priceless counselling, as often as she needed.

Mrs Banerjee wanted to teach ladies to speak in English, so that they could forge ahead in life. He made it possible for her by gifting her books, helping her in her time management. Now over the past 35 years, she has her own Institute for Spoken English for men & women of any profession.

Along with many other things she did, she started her workshops on Thought Management, Listening & Communication skills, Creating Confidence & something very close to her heart, 'Parenting, a lifetime project'. He was instrumental in making all this come true.

Her son is her sounding board. He has always been a source of inspiration for her. No matter how complicated the issue might seem, he has a way of first listening & then giving a simple logical solution.

Daughter is always a source of pride. Extremely talented & resourceful, she helped in actually getting the ideas executed. Without her guidance, this project could never get completed.

The author says, "I feel immensely grateful to God for blessing me with such a wonderful family. My family gave me the real insight to life & that is how, I had the courage to pen down my thoughts in the form of this book."

Mrs Surabhi Banerjee, MSc, Botany was awarded a UGC Scholarship.

She is also a Reiki Master, a Silva Mind Control graduate, has undergone Vipassana training and is an Accredited Trainer & Counsellor from the Dynamic Living Institute in UK.

Acknowledgements

I had never thought in my life, that I would have the patience to pen down my observations. I realise now, there are life defining moments in every person's life, which then lead him on a path totally unknown to him, yet, when travelled it is so satisfying.

When I look back, there are so many faces that come to my mind, who played a vital role in making my book a reality. I would like to thank each one of them.

My mother, Late Mrs Arati Maitra who shaped my thoughts & made me the person I am today . Long back then, it was considered a taboo to enrol a girl child in an English medium Convent school. My mother had the foresight & courage to fight against the social norms & enrol me in a Convent School. Had she not taken this decision, I would never have the desire to write in English or have the courage to teach English to professionals who wish to converse in English but can't .Dear Maa, you will always remain as the most loved & respected person in my life.

My father Mr. Anil Chandra Maitra, always a guiding force & support, who encouraged me to write, what I believed in.

My husband Alok, who showed immense patience, throughout the period, when I was putting together so many things & needed his help all the time . He was there to bail me out, whenever I got stuck.

My daughter Anushree, my friend, philosopher and guide . I wish everyone was blessed with a daughter like her. A great solution provider. She provided me with solutions to every problem that I faced, was a constant source of encouragement. I feel I can do nothing without her.

Son Amit, taught me to do whatever I decided to do, with a relaxed attitude .Always helped in reducing my tension.

My best friend, Nutan Sathe, who never doubted my capabilities, always tried to understand my viewpoint and re-assured me that I can do it.

My friend, Suresh Kamath, more of a brother, spent time, listening to the chapters, read out by me and gave me his positive feedback, which meant a lot.

My branding partner, Mr Arjun Samaddar of Reve Consulting Pvt. Ltd.(India) – gave his priceless guidance related to the different aspects of the book.

My IPR lawyer, Gauri Bhave, who got the Copyright registration of my book, done very efficiently.

All the students of my Institute, who eagerly listened to me, when I read out different chapters to them and encouraged me to complete the book.

Last but not the least, my dearest nephew, Late Chandan Banerjee, whose beautiful hand drawn greeting card on our first wedding anniversary, has now become the cover of this book.

Printed in the United States
By Bookmasters